SHOW'S OVER

Jamie Michalak

CANDLEWICK
ENTERTAINMENT

Major funding for *Fetch!* is provided by the National Science Foundation and public-television viewers.
This *Fetch!* material is based upon work supported by the National Science Foundation
under Grant No. 0813513. Any opinions, findings, and conclusions
or recommendations expressed in this material are those of the author(s)
and do not necessarily reflect the views of the National Science Foundation.

First edition 2014

Library of Congress Catalog Card Number 2012950640
ISBN 978-0-7636-7278-2 (hardcover)
ISBN 978-0-7636-6809-9 (paperback)

14 15 16 17 18 19 SWT 10 9 8 7 6 5 4 3 2 1

Printed in Dongguan, Guangdong, China

This book was typeset in Adobe Caslon Semibold.
The illustrations were created digitally.

Candlewick Entertainment
An imprint of Candlewick Press
99 Dover Street
Somerville, Massachusetts 02144

visit us at www.candlewick.com

CONTENTS

You're invited to the

**Poodle
Ball**

CHAPTER ONE
Ha Ha

One morning, Ruff Ruffman, host of the game show *FETCH!*, received an invitation. He snatched it up. It was an invitation to the Poodle Ball from Charlene, the poodle next door. Ruff used to have a crush on Charlene . . . and still did.

Ruff read the note at the bottom of the invitation about the dress code for the ball. "I have to wear fancy pants," he said.

"Good thing I always have my fancy pants right here in my — *what?*"

The hanger was empty. "Someone swiped my *fancy pants?*"

"I bet if I tell Charlene I've lost my fancy pants, she'll take Spot Spotnik to the ball instead!"

No pants, no ball, no date with Charlene. What could be worse?

Just then, Ruff and Blossom heard a fax coming through. Ruff snatched it off the machine and read it out loud:

"Fax to: Mr. Ruffman

You're fired!

Ha Ha."

"I'm OK. Really," he said. "I've had worse days than this. It's no . . . big . . . WAAHHHH!"

Blossom handed Ruff a tissue. Then she held up the fax and pointed to the "Ha Ha."

"Maybe it's all a joke," Ruff said.

Blossom nodded.

"Or not!" Ruff said, grabbing the newspaper, which had also just arrived. What a lot of news for one day! "This says our TV station was just bought by the richest woman in Australia, Harriet Hackensack!"

Ruff circled the first two letters of her first and last names: Ha Ha.

"Hackensack never leaves her hotel room," he read. "She's rich and . . . *hates dogs*! How can anyone hate dogs?"

Ruff scratched his side while he read, sending fleas flying. Blossom winced.

"So that's why Hackensack fired me," he said. "She just hates dogs. I'm sure she would change her mind if she actually met me. . . . What's not to like?"

Ruff came up with a plan: go to Australia and change Hackensack's mind about the show, then find some new fancy pants so he could go to the ball with Charlene.

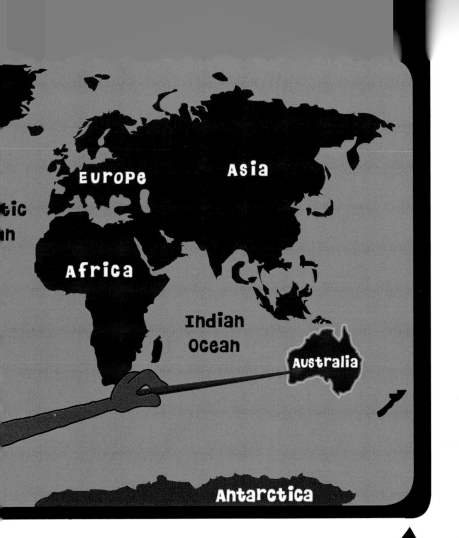

Europe

Asia

Africa

Indian
Ocean

Australia

Antarctica

Blossom thought the whole thing seemed a bit far-*fetch*ed but agreed to go along with it.

CHAPTER TWO
Egg-Roll Power

Now that Ruff and Blossom had a plan to go to Australia, it was time for action! How would they get there? Too bad Blossom was just sitting around reading a boring-looking book called *Green Machines: How to Convert Your Doghouse into an Environmentally Sustainable Vehicle on the Cheap.*

Ruff decided to find Chet, his mouse assistant. Chet lives in a swanky mouse hole in the Fetch 3000, the computer that helps run the show *FETCH!*

"Chet has probably already come up with a plan to get us to Australia!" Ruff said. "Chet!"

Just then, Chet scurried out of his hole carrying some Chinese food.

"Chet!" Ruff said, picking up an egg roll. "You dropped something."

Blossom grabbed it.

"You want it?" Ruff asked.

Blossom pointed to her book.

"Green machines run on wind power, solar energy, or used cooking oil," Ruff said. "Um, that's great, Blossom, but . . . Wait! *Oil!* The Chinese restaurant keeps used oil in their back alley. We'll go to Australia using the power of Chinese food. Chet is a genius!"

Blossom rolled her eyes.

Ruff, Blossom, and Chet worked day and night to turn Ruff's doghouse into a green machine.

Finally, it was time to boogie.

"So long, backyard!" Ruff called, driving into the ocean. "Hello, Australia!"

Blossom tapped Ruff's shoulder.

"Not now," he said. "I'm driving the first
doghouse submarine-car."

Blossom waved the blueprints.

"What? We forgot the submarine part?"

he said. "That means —"

Water began to fill the doghouse. "AAGH!
Chet, help!" Ruff yelled.

Instead, Chet just pushed over a crate of pineapples.

"Chet, this is no time for a snack," Ruff said.

Then Blossom began tying the pineapples around the doghouse. "Why are you decorating this sinking doghouse with fruit?" he asked her.

Then Ruff saw that the pineapples were keeping the green machine afloat.

"Pineapples float!" he said. "Chet, you're brilliant!"

And . . . a month later, they reached Australia. Crikey!

CHAPTER THREE
Jazz Paws!

"Here it is, Hackensack's Hotel," Ruff said at the gates.

Blossom pointed to the No Dogs Allowed sign.

"How will I get in, then?" Ruff asked.

And that's how Ruff ended up squeezed into a pink cat costume.

Blossom helped Ruff practice some cat moves, like:

pouncing . . .

Boing!

licking . . .

Cough.

Patoooey!

Yuck.

and leaping . . .

Whee!

BANG! Oof!

Next they rolled a food cart to Hackensack's room. Chet hid behind a covered dish.

"Room service!" Ruff announced, stepping inside.

Hackensack was sitting by the fire. "I wasn't expecting room service," she said.

Ruff whipped out some roses.

"Nor were you expecting flowers from a do — a do —" He tugged at the zipper of his cat suit. It was stuck. "Er, just a moment."

"What's going on?" Hackensack said.

"Police!"

"Try Plan B, Blossom!" Ruff cried. "Jazz paws!"

Blossom lifted the dish cover to reveal her radio.

The room filled with smooth jazz.

"We're a couple of cats from Kalamazoo!"
Ruff sang.

Blossom and Ruff tap-danced across the room. *Tappity-tap* . . . right into a vase. *Crash!*

Hackensack looked angry.

"I don't know who you two are," she

snarled, "but what you just did was . . .

fantastic!" she cried.

"Really?" Ruff asked, relieved. "Well, I *am* actually Ruff Ruffman, the star of—"

"Not you, clumsy cat," she snapped. She pointed to Blossom. "*You*, the quiet lad." Then she turned to Ruff. "You can leave. Now. GUARDS!"

CHAPTER FOUR
The Secret of
the Fancy Pants

"Our trip was a bust, Chet," Ruff said back at home. "*FETCH!* is going off the air, Spot is going to go to the ball with Charlene, and I'm still trapped in this cat suit. The worst part is that Blossom took a job with Hackensack, so now I don't even have a show supervisor. But I guess that's OK since I don't even have a show. . . . WAAHHHH!" Ruff sobbed.

Somebody poked Ruff's back.

"Blossom!" Ruff cried. "What are you doing here?"

Ruff found out the whole story from Blossom: she took the job with Hackensack to get Ruff his job back—but she found out that it wasn't Harriet Hackensack who sent that fax!

"You mean she's not Ha Ha?" Ruff asked.

"Then the fax *is* a joke! That means *FETCH!*
is still on the air. Hooray!"

And then Ruff found out that Blossom had
seen Spot Spotnick walking around town in
Ruff's fancy pants!

"So *he* swiped them!" Ruff said. "He must have sent that fax, too, just to get me out of town so he could be Charlene's date tonight!"

But what Spotnik didn't know about Ruff's pants was that they were so fancy, they could self-destruct by remote control.

"Ha, ha," Ruff said, pressing a button on the Fetch 3000. A message flashed across its screen:

The next day, Spot made front-page news: "Spot Spotnik Loses Pants at Poodle Ball."

Now, if only they could figure out how to get Ruff out of the cat suit. . . .

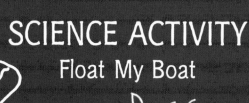

SCIENCE ACTIVITY
Float My Boat

A boat's shape and size determine how much it can carry. Build a few aluminum-foil boats and test different designs. How many pennies can you load without sinking your boat?

WHAT YOU'LL NEED:

three or more 6-inch squares of aluminum foil

some pennies

a ruler

a large bowl half-filled with water

WHAT TO DO:

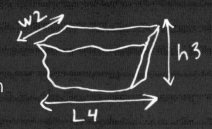

1. <u>Make a boat.</u>

   Mold a square of aluminum foil into a boat shape.

   Record its length, width, and height on a data table.

2. Make a prediction.

How many pennies do you think your boat can hold before it sinks?

3. Float your boat.

Place your empty boat in a container of water. Add pennies one at a time. Keep going until the boat sinks, then record how many pennies it held. But don't count the last one — since it sank the boat!

4. Try some different designs.

Make a total of three boats with different shapes. You can keep making new designs, using what you learned about the height and thickness of the sides, the size of the bottom, and how to position the pennies. Record your designs, predictions, and test results in the data table.

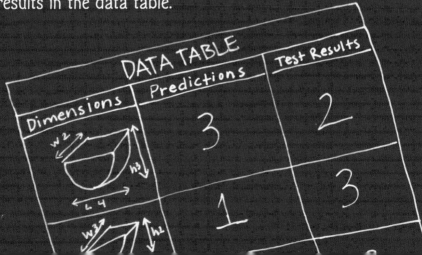

DATA TABLE

Dimensions	Predictions	Test Results
	3	2
		3
	1	

CHEW ON THIS!

When a boat floats, it settles into the water, pushing the water aside to make room for itself. But it's a two-way pushing match—the water pushes back on the bottom and sides of the boat. This force, called buoyancy, holds the boat up. The more water a boat pushes aside, the more force there will be pushing back on the boat and supporting it. This is why a boat's size and shape make such a difference in how much of a load it can carry without sinking.

S.S. FETCH

GOOOO FETCH!